Tia
the Tulip
Fairy

To Lily Grace Evans,
who will always believe in fairies

Special thanks to Sue Mongredien

ISBN-10: 0-545-07090-2
ISBN-13: 978-0-545-07090-4

12 11 10 9 8 7 6 5 4 3 2 1   9 10 11 12 13/0

Printed in China

First Scholastic Printing, February 2009

Tia
the Tulip
Fairy

by Daisy Meadows

SCHOLASTIC INC.

New York Toronto London Auckland Sydney
Mexico City New Delhi Hong Kong Buenos Aires

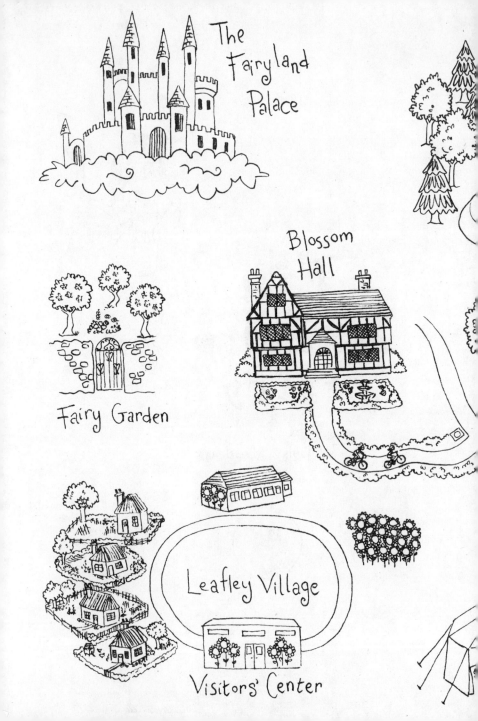

The Fairyland Palace

Blossom Hall

Fairy Garden

Leafley Village

Visitors' Center

I need the magic petals' powers,
To give my castle garden flowers.
I plan to use my magic well
To work against the fairies' spell

From my wand ice magic flies,
Frosty bolts through fairy skies.
This is the crafty spell I weave
To bring the petals back to me.

Contents

A Fairy Garden

"I think the Fairy Garden must be through here," Rachel Walker said, pointing to an iron gate. She and her friend Kirsty Tate were exploring the grounds of Blossom Hall, an old hotel where their families were staying for spring vacation. Both girls had been interested to hear the owner of Blossom

Hall, Mrs. Forrest, talk as she'd served their breakfast that morning. She told them about the history of the hotel. It once had been a large house with a very special garden — a fairy garden. This caught the girls' attention. After all, Kirsty and Rachel knew a lot about fairies: They were friends with them!

"It's known as the Fairy Garden because there is a perfect ring of tulips growing in the middle of it," Mrs. Forrest had explained. "We call it the Blossom Fairy Ring. And you've come at just the right time of year. The tulips are

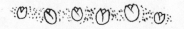

blooming and they look beautiful,
though I don't think they're as bright as
they were last year."

As soon as they'd finished their
breakfast, Rachel and Kirsty had asked
their parents if it was all right for them to
go exploring. The families had arrived at
Blossom Hall the night before, and the
girls were excited to look around in the
warmth of the morning sun. From the
breakfast room, the
gardens looked very
pretty. They had
pink-and-white
flowering cherry
trees, long
rolling lawns,
and clusters of
cheerful flowers.

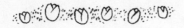

"Of course you can explore," Mr. Tate had said. "Just make sure you stay inside the wall that runs around Blossom Hall and its gardens."

Mrs. Forrest had told the girls to follow the winding path that led through a group of trees at the back of the house.

"You'll come to a walled garden, with a gate on one side," she'd said. "The Fairy Garden is in there."

The girls followed Mrs. Forrest's directions, and now Rachel lifted the latch of the gate eagerly. "Here we are!" she said, pushing it open.

The girls stepped into the walled garden together. "It's beautiful!" Kirsty exclaimed, taking in the rambling roses that climbed the walls and the old stone fountain in one corner.

"It's just the kind of place you can imagine a real fairy visiting," Rachel said, smiling. "And that must be the Blossom Fairy Ring!" she added, pointing to a circle of yellow and orange tulips. The bright flowers grew in a grassy area at the very middle of the peaceful little garden.

"How pretty!" Kirsty said. She walked

over for a closer look and noticed that
some of the tulips were
wilting. She stopped
and listened
carefully. "Rachel,
do you hear
someone crying?"
she asked in a
whisper.

Rachel stood
still, listening
hard, then
nodded. She also
heard the faint sound of sobs.
"But I don't see anyone else here," she
whispered back. "Who could it be?"

The girls looked around the small
garden. It wasn't big enough to have
many hiding places. Then, as Kirsty was

walking past the tulips in the fairy ring, she paused. The crying was definitely louder there. It seemed to be coming from the tulips themselves.

Kirsty looked inside the nearest tulip and gasped. A tiny fairy was sitting at the bottom of the flower, with her face in her hands.

Kirsty motioned to Rachel, then kneeled down by the flower. "Hello,"

she said gently. "I'm
Kirsty. What's
the matter?"

The fairy gave a
gulp and looked up
at Kirsty. She had
long brown wavy
hair, and was wearing
a cute white-and-
orange outfit with a pretty
tulip necklace and little orange shoes.

"Hello," she said sadly. "I'm Tia the
Tulip Fairy, and I'm looking for my
magic petal."

"Hi, Tia," said Rachel, crouching next
to Kirsty. "Maybe we can help you find
the petal?" she suggested. "We've helped
lots of other fairies before."

Tia looked from Rachel to Kirsty, and her face brightened. "Rachel and Kirsty? I've heard all about you," she said. "Oh, thank goodness you're here!"

Kirsty smiled. "What happened to your petal?" she asked. "How did you lose it?"

Tia got to her feet. "It's a long story. I might need some help explaining," she said. As she spoke, she sprinkled a handful of orange, petal-shaped fairy dust over the girls. Before they knew it, they found themselves

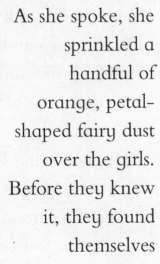

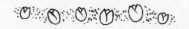

shrinking until they were the same size
as Tia.

"We're fairies!" exclaimed Rachel,
fluttering the shimmering wings on her
back with delight. Then she noticed that
the Fairy Garden was blurring right
before her eyes.

She had just enough time to grab
Kirsty's hand before she felt herself being
pulled quickly through the air. "Where
are we going?" she cried, feeling a rush
of excitement.

"To Fairyland, of course!" Tia called
back with a smile.

Petal Thieves

After a few moments, the girls felt
themselves slowing down, and then they
landed on the ground. They were
standing in front of the Fairyland palace.
Its towers and turrets gleamed in the
sunshine. Nearby stood the king and
queen of Fairyland, along with a group

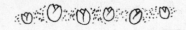

of other fairies that Kirsty and Rachel
did not recognize.

"Hello, Your Majesties," Kirsty said,
giving a polite curtsey. She and Rachel
had been to Fairyland many times to
help the fairies, but she was still filled
with awe every time she saw King
Oberon and Queen Titania.

The king and queen both smiled.

"We're so glad to see you again," the
king told the girls.

"You're just in time to help," the queen
added.

"What happened?" Rachel
asked.

The smile slipped
from the king's face.
"I'm afraid Jack Frost
has been up to his
tricks again," he said
seriously. "This time,
he's been causing trouble
for our Petal Fairies."

Rachel and Kirsty exchanged glances.
Jack Frost was always up to no good in
the fairy world.

"What has he done now?" Kirsty
asked, raising her eyebrows.

"He was upset that none of the beautiful
flowers of Fairyland would grow around
his cold ice castle," the queen explained.
"So he sent his goblins to steal the Petal
Fairies' magic petals, hoping that their
powerful petal magic would help."

"Here are our Petal Fairies," the king
said, introducing them one by one.
"You've met Tia the Tulip Fairy, and
this is Pippa the Poppy Fairy, Louise the
Lily Fairy, Charlotte the Sunflower
Fairy, Olivia the Orchid Fairy, Danielle
the Daisy Fairy, and
Ella the Rose
Fairy."

The Petal
Fairies all gave
small smiles of
welcome, but
Kirsty and
Rachel couldn't
help noticing
how sad they
looked.

"Let's go to the seeing pool," the queen

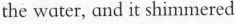

suggested. "We can show you how it all happened."

The girls followed the fairies through the palace gardens to the magical seeing pool. The queen waved her wand over the water, and it shimmered with all the colors of the rainbow as a picture formed on its surface. Kirsty and Rachel stared at the images forming in the pool. There, they saw a group of Jack Frost's goblins sneaking into the palace gardens. The sun was just rising, and one of the goblins was yawning.

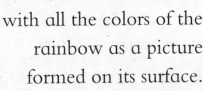

"That's our home," Tia told the girls, pointing out a tall pagoda. The goblins

were creeping toward the pretty pink
building. It was four stories high, with little
golden balconies and a sparkling golden
roof. "We sleep on the top three floors."

"The ground floor is where we keep
the magic petals,"
Charlotte added.

"Where we *kept*
them, you
mean," Olivia
said sadly.
"Until this
morning . . ."

The girls
watched as the
goblins tiptoed into
the pagoda. Moments
later, they appeared again.
They now had gleeful smiles on their faces

19

and seven colorful petals, each the size of
a small pancake, in their hands.

"Jack Frost is going to be so happy
with us when we bring these back to the
ice castle," the first goblin cackled,
waving an orange petal above his head
in triumph.

Tia let out a groan as she watched.
"That's my magic petal. Look at the
way he's whirling it around!" she cried.
"He's not taking good care of it at all!"

Rachel squeezed
Tia's hand to
try to comfort
her as they
watched what
happened.
The other
goblins all

looked amazed as a stream of orange
tulips floated out from Tia's magic petal.
The tulips planted themselves in the
ground under a tree!

"Hey!" shouted one goblin with an
especially long nose. "How did you
do that?"

The goblin with the orange petal
stopped and stared at the clumps of tulips
that had appeared. "I just . . . waved it,"
he said in surprise. "Like this." He shook
the petal again, and another stream of

tulips — pink ones this
time — appeared. These
flowers planted themselves
nearby, too.

"Wow!" the long-
nosed goblin
exclaimed. He
held the yellow
petal in his
hand and
looked at it
with curiosity.

"That's mine,"
Charlotte the
Sunflower Fairy
told Kirsty and
Rachel, frowning.

The long-nosed goblin
wiggled the yellow petal, and

seconds later, a bunch of
sunflowers sprang up at
his feet. He jumped
back in surprise
and then
chuckled.
"This is
great!" he
said with
excitement.
"Where else
can we grow
flowers?"
Before
long, all the
goblins were
playing around with
the magic petals. Purple
flowers popped up around tree

trunks, red ones blossomed in a nearby
stream, and a big white daisy appeared
on one goblin's head!

The queen shook her head as she
watched from the side of the seeing pool.
"And while those goblins were playing
with the petal magic," she said
disapprovingly, "our Petal Fairies woke
up and realized that their petals had been
stolen."

"And we wanted them back!" Ella the
Rose Fairy declared.

"When the magic
petals are safe
inside the
pagoda,"
Louise the
Lily Fairy

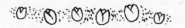

explained, "our
wands are
automatically
filled with
petal magic
each morning.
Of course, that
didn't happen this morning because the
petals were gone, but we still had a little
petal magic left. So we used the last drops
to make a spell that would bring the
magic petals back to us."

In the pool, Kirsty and Rachel could
see the effect of the fairies' spell. The
petals were swept out of the goblins'
hands. A magic wind carried them back
toward the fairies in a sparkly, pink
stream, high in the air.

The goblins looked alarmed. "Quick,
get them back!" one of the goblins
shouted. He rushed after the petals.

The others followed, running along
and jumping up, trying to grab the
floating petals. "Jack Frost will be angry
if he finds out we let them go!" one of
the goblins panted.

"He certainly will!" boomed a chilling

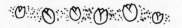

voice. Just then, Kirsty and Rachel saw
that Jack Frost had appeared behind the
goblins. He looked furious.

Jack Frost muttered a few magic words.
Then he waved his wand in the air,
shooting an icy bolt of magic straight
toward the petals.

Goblins Get Magic

Boom! Jack Frost's icy magic collided with the fairies' petal magic. There was an enormous explosion of pink petals and dazzling white-and-silver snowflakes. The magic petals flew in all directions like sparks. Then they disappeared from view.

"Where did they go?" Rachel asked.

The Petal Fairies exchanged glances.

"That's the problem," Tia replied.

"They're lost in the human world," the king explained. "But we don't know where!"

"We'll help you find them," Kirsty said at once. She felt chills at the thought of another fairy adventure.

The king and queen smiled at the girls.

"We were hoping you'd say that,"
the queen said warmly. "Without the
petals, the Petal Fairies can't make
new flowers grow."

"And when they don't have their
petals, all the flowers already in bloom
die more quickly," the
king added sadly.

"That's awful,"
Kirsty said. She
could hardly
imagine what
the world would
look like without
flowers. The
gardens of Blossom
Hall would seem empty,
and her own garden at home would no
longer be full of color!

"We'll do our best to help you get the magic petals back," Rachel promised the Petal Fairies.

The queen waved her wand over the seeing pool again. "There's just one more thing we need to show you before you go. . . ."

Kirsty and Rachel watched the pool as colors rippled across the surface. The picture changed. Now they saw Jack Frost in the great hall of his ice castle, demanding that his goblins find the magic petals.

"I order you to stay together," he told the goblins firmly. "Do whatever you have to do to bring the petals back to me. That includes using this. . . ." He handed a magic wand to the goblin closest to him. The goblin took the glittering silver wand, a mischievous grin spreading across his face.

"This wand is charged with my own powerful magic," Jack Frost explained. "I'm giving it to you to make sure you don't get outwitted by those fairies again. Don't let me down!"

The goblins all nodded eagerly.

"You must take great care," the king warned Kirsty and Rachel as the picture faded. "The goblins will be in one big group, and they will have a wand full of Jack Frost's magic. They could get into all kinds of trouble." Rachel nodded solemnly. "We'll be careful," she promised, biting her lip.

Just then, Tia stepped forward. "I thought I could sense my tulip petal near Blossom Hall — that's why I was there this morning," she explained. "Maybe we could look there first?"

"Of course," Kirsty said.

Pippa the Poppy Fairy nodded. "Once that petal has been found, at least the tulips will be safe," she said. She turned to the girls. "Each petal protects its own particular flower and flowers of a certain color," she told them. "So Tia's orange petal not only makes the tulips grow, but also every other orange-colored flower — like marigolds. When all seven magic petals are safe in Fairyland, they make all the flowers in the world grow!"

Kirsty and Rachel turned back to Tia. "What are we waiting for?" Rachel asked, grinning.

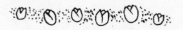

"Let's go back to Blossom Hall and start searching!" Kirsty added.

Tia smiled gratefully. Then she waved her wand, sending a flurry of fairy dust swirling all around the three of them. Kirsty and Rachel had just enough time to wave good-bye to the king, queen, and the Petal Fairies before they were swept up in a whirl of glittering color.

The girls were off on another exciting fairy adventure!

It's Raining Petals!

When the magic whirlwind came to a stop, Rachel and Kirsty found themselves standing on one of the lawns of Blossom Hall. They were girls again.

Tia fluttered in front of them. "Let's start looking!" the little fairy called, her wings a shimmering blur as she flew toward the nearest flowerbed. "I'm sure

the magic tulip petal is somewhere close.
I can just feel it."

The three of them began searching a
row of flowerbeds — Tia from the air,
Rachel and Kirsty walking carefully along
the edge — all hoping to spot the bright
orange petal. Kirsty couldn't help noticing
that some of the flowers were looking
wilted, and there were a few empty spots
where nothing was growing at all.

Tia noticed Kirsty staring at the bare
patches of earth. "There should be some
lilies coming up there," she told the girls,
"but they haven't started growing yet,
because the lily petal is lost." She
pointed to another empty patch. "Soon,
there should be some gorgeous poppies
over there," she said, looking sad again.
"But if Pippa doesn't get her
poppy petal back,
then . . ." her voice
trailed off.

Rachel stared at
the bare ground,
feeling sad. They
had to find the magic
petals — the sooner
the better!

Once they'd
checked all the
flowerbeds, the girls
and Tia headed
over to a rock
garden. Unfortunately,
there was no sign
of the magic tulip petal
there, and they didn't
see it anywhere by the
trickling fountains.

"There's an apple
orchard," Kirsty said,
pointing. "Should we try
looking there?"

"Good idea," Rachel said, walking
toward it. "Oh, aren't the trees beautiful
with all their blossoms?"

The others agreed. Delicate sprays of

pinky-white flowers lined the branches of the apple trees.

"And that one is even prettier than the others," Kirsty said, pointing out a tree a short distance away. It was covered in blossoms. "I wonder why it's flowering so well?" A thought struck her and she stopped. Kirsty looked excitedly at Tia. "You don't think it has anything to do with your petal's magic powers, do you?"

Tia's eyes lit up. "It might, Kirsty. Let's take a closer look!" she said.

Tia and the girls hurried toward the tree, but they came to a sudden halt when they spotted Jack Frost's band of goblins underneath it!

The goblins were all shaking the trunk of the tree as hard as they could. Showers of apple blossoms tumbled from the branches like confetti.

"Why are they doing that?" Rachel
wondered aloud.

"My petal! It's there, in the tree!" Tia
cried suddenly, pointing to a high branch.

Rachel and Kirsty looked up and
noticed a bright orange petal stuck in the
highest branches of the tree. The magic
petal was much larger than a real petal,
Kirsty noticed. It was almost as big as her
own hand.

"They're shaking the tree to try to get the petal loose," Rachel gasped. "We've got to get it before they do!"

Tia waved her wand over the girls, and Rachel and Kirsty began to shrink. They became fairies again!

"Let's try and fly up to the petal without the goblins seeing us," Tia suggested. "But watch out for the falling blossoms!"

"Okay," Kirsty said, fluttering her wings. "Let's go!"

She and Rachel followed their fairy friend as she easily dodged the falling

petals. *It's just like*
flying through a
blizzard of sweet-
smelling snowflakes,
Rachel thought, as
she zoomed upward.

"Keep shaking!" one of the goblins
shouted from down below, still rocking
the tree trunk. "It's got to fall soon!"

"Not if we can get it first," Kirsty
muttered, fluttering her wings faster than
ever. She, Rachel, and Tia were closing
in on the petal, but just then, Kirsty
heard a loud shout.

"Hey! What's that up there?"

Kirsty glanced down to see a bunch of
nasty goblin faces glaring up at her. She'd
been spotted!

A Silly Spell

The three fairies flew up to the petal,
grabbed hold of it, and tried to pull it
away from the tree. But it was stuck to
a twig.

Rachel could see that one of the
goblins was pointing Jack Frost's wand
up at them.

"I think we should try this wand out,"

he said to his friends. "Anyone know any good spells?"

"Just make something up!" another goblin advised. "Say something that sounds magical."

"Let's try shaking the petal loose," Tia urged quickly. "I don't like the sound of this!"

The three fairies jiggled and shook the soft, smooth petal until it suddenly broke free from the twig.

"Let's go!" Rachel cried.

But before they could fly away with the petal, the goblin with the wand started chanting.

"Pesky fairies, that's enough! I conjure up a . . ." he paused, his face turning doubtful. "What should I conjure up?" he asked his friends.

"A wind that's rough!" shouted a goblin with mean eyes.

"No chance," Tia spluttered. "I've never heard such an awful spell!"

"It might be an awful spell, Tia," Rachel said anxiously. "But I think it's working!"

The three fairies all cried out in alarm
as a stream of icy wind flooded from Jack
Frost's wand straight toward them. As
it reached the fairies, it swept them
high into the air.

"Hold on tight to the
petal!" Kirsty shouted, but
the wind whipped the
words from her mouth,
and then ripped the petal
right out of her hands.

Rachel and Tia found it
impossible to cling
on to the edges of
the petal, too,
and the three
fairies were
thrown into

the branches of
another tree.

They watched
helplessly as the
wind carried the
tulip petal up and
away from them,
higher and higher.
Soon it was just a dot in the sky.

Kirsty leaned against the branch she'd
landed on, trying to catch her breath.
She wondered what they should do now.
The petal was gone, and they couldn't
possibly fly after it in such a storm.

After a few moments, the spell wore off
and the wind died down.

"Are you two all right?" Tia asked
Kirsty and Rachel. The girls nodded, and

Tia sighed with relief. "That wand is more powerful than I'd thought," she said. "Where did it send my petal?"

The three fairies scoured the sky, hoping to catch a glimpse of the orange petal, but they couldn't see any sign of it. Then Rachel noticed that the goblins on the ground were acting strange. They

were running in circles, staring at the
sky. She glanced up to see what they
were looking at, and saw the petal way
above them. It was floating down from a
great height, drifting back and forth on
the breeze.

"Look! The goblins spotted it!" Rachel
cried to the others. "Quick!"

The three fairies
zoomed toward the
falling petal, hoping
to catch it before it
fell into a goblin's
hand. But once
again, the goblins saw
them coming.
"Cast another spell!" they urged the
one with the wand.

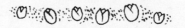

Kirsty braced herself as he pointed the wand up toward the fairies and shouted out another spell.

"Let's have an icy gale again. Blow, wind, blow, when I count to ten!"

Then he stood there, looking pleased with himself, until one of the other goblins nudged him. "Go on, then!" he yelled. "Count to ten, you fool!"

"Oh, yes," the first goblin muttered. "One, two, three, four, five, six, seven-eight-nine-ten!" he counted at top speed. Then, "Go!" he shouted with a loud cackle.

The Wrong End of the Stick

Rachel braced herself, waiting for the freezing blast of wind to strike a second time. She could hardly look, knowing she was about to be swept away all over again.

But then, to her surprise, she heard Kirsty and Tia giggling. Rachel looked at her friends, and then followed their gaze to see what they were laughing at. They were watching the goblins.

Once again, an icy wind was streaming from the wand, but this time it wasn't blowing toward the fairies. The goblin hadn't realized that he was pointing the wand in the wrong

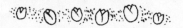

direction, so the wind that he'd meant for
the fairies was actually blowing right at
him and his goblin friends!

"Help!" they cried, as the windstorm
swept them up and sent them tumbling
along the ground. "What's happening?"

Kirsty cheered. She and her two friends

swooped down to the magic petal, which
had just landed on the grass. Tia waved
her wand, shrinking the petal to its

Fairyland size.
Then she whizzed
up into the air
with the petal in
her hand, doing
a figure eight
in delight.
"It's wonderful
to have my
petal back!"
She beamed.
"Thank you
so much for
helping me, girls!"
"Any time," Rachel said, smiling.
"We're happy to help, Tia."

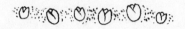

"I'd better take my petal back to
Fairyland now," Tia said. "My sisters
will be so pleased!" She flew above Kirsty
and Rachel, showering them with
orange fairy dust and turning them back
into girls again.

"Thanks again,"
Tia sang. "See
you soon!"

"Good-bye, Tia,"
Kirsty called, as the
little fairy
disappeared in a
shimmer of orange
magic.

"That was fun," Rachel said happily as
she and Kirsty headed back through the
orchard.

"Yes it was," Kirsty agreed. "But I

hope the goblins don't get any better at casting spells. I don't like that they have a magic wand to use now."

The girls left the orchard and headed along a path toward the hotel. As they walked past a large flowering bush, they heard angry voices. Curious, they peeked into the bush — and saw all of the goblins tangled in a heap!

Kirsty and Rachel looked at each other and burst out laughing. "It's going to take them a while to get out of there," Kirsty giggled.

The two friends were crossing the lawn toward Blossom Hall when Rachel suddenly stopped walking and nudged Kirsty. "Kirsty, look," she said, pointing at one of the flowerbeds. "Those tulips look a little perkier than when we were here earlier."

Kirsty turned to see. Her friend was right. The tulips were all standing up proudly now, looking much brighter and

healthier than they had before. She
grinned. "Tia's magic must be working
already!" she said in a low voice. "And
look at the orange ones. They definitely
weren't there before."

"They're beautiful," Rachel said.

"There are still lots of bare patches in the garden, though," Kirsty pointed out. "I really hope we can find the other magic petals soon."

Rachel nodded. "One thing's for sure," she said, linking arms with her friend. "We're in for a very exciting week!"

THE PETAL FAIRIES

Tia the Tulip Fairy has
her magic petal back. Now Rachel
and Kirsty must help

Pippa

the Poppy Fairy!

Take a look at their next adventure
in this special sneak peek!

"I love Blossom Hall!" Kirsty Tate sighed
happily as she finished off a delicious
bowl of fruit and cereal.

She was sitting on the sunny terrace of
the hotel restaurant with her best friend,
Rachel Walker, and their parents. The
two families were spending spring break
at the beautiful old mansion that was

now a hotel. The sky was blue, and the pink-and-white cherry trees in the gardens were in full bloom.

"It's so pretty," Rachel agreed.

"Did you find the Fairy Garden yesterday?" Mrs. Tate asked.

"It was magical!" Rachel said. She and Kirsty grinned at each other.

"What do you two want to do today?" asked Mr. Walker.

"We'd like to explore inside Blossom Hall," Rachel said eagerly.

"I can't wait to look around," Kirsty added. "Mom, can we please —"

"Yes, you can leave the table if you've finished." Mrs. Tate laughed.

Rachel and Kirsty left the restaurant and headed down one of the winding hallways.

The girls arrived in the hotel lobby, a spacious room with stained glass windows and a large wooden table. Just then, the main doors opened and a man in a blue uniform came in, carrying an enormous basket of flowers.

Rachel stared at the flowers. Suddenly her heart skipped a beat. "Kirsty," she whispered, "I just saw some red fairy sparkles shoot out of the basket!"

"Oh!" Kirsty looked thrilled.

The two girls hurried over to the flowers. As they reached them, there was another shower of crimson sparkles, and a tiny fairy zoomed out from the middle of a scarlet poppy.